THESE ARE THE CHORES WE DO

Retold by BLAKE HOENA

Illustrated by DOREEN MARTS

CANTATA
LEARNING

WWW.CANTATALEARNING.COM

CANTATA
LEARNING

Published by Cantata Learning
1710 Roe Crest Drive
North Mankato, MN 56003
www.cantatalearning.com

Library of Congress Control Number: 2015932818
Hoena, Blake
　　These Are the Chores We Do / retold by Blake Hoena; Illustrated by Doreen Marts
　　Series: Tangled Tunes
　　Audience: Ages: 3–8; Grades: PreK–3
　　Summary: It takes some work to get ready for the day. But this twist on the classic
song "Here We Go Round the Mulberry Bush" makes chores fun.
　　ISBN: 978-1-63290-365-5 (library binding/CD)
　　ISBN: 978-1-63290-496-6 (paperback/CD)
　　ISBN: 978-1-63290-526-0 (paperback)
　　1. Stories in rhyme. 2. Chores—fiction. 3. Monsters—fiction.

Book design and art direction, Tim Palin Creative
Editorial direction, Flat Sole Studio
Music direction, Elizabeth Draper
Music arranged and produced by Drew Temperante

Printed in the United States of America in North Mankato, Minnesota.
122015　　0326CGS16

ACCESS THE MUSIC!

SCAN CODE WITH MOBILE APP

CANTATALEARNING.COM

Chores are jobs or tasks that you need to do. They may include putting your toys away or feeding your pets. The monsters in this story have chores they do every day. What sorts of chores do you have to do?

Now turn the page and sing about doing chores!

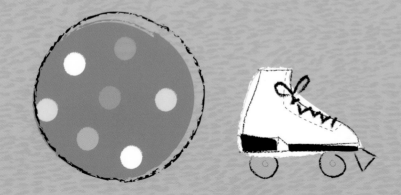

Every day there are chores to do.
So get them done and have some fun.

Now this is the way we make our bed,
make our bed, make our bed.

This is the way we make our bed
so early every morning.

This is the way we tie our shoes,
tie our shoes, tie our shoes.

This is the way we tie our shoes
so early Monday morning.

Every day there are chores to do.
So get them done and have some fun.

Now, this is the way we zip our coat,
zip our coat, zip our coat.

This is the way we zip our coat
so early Tuesday morning.

This is the way we feed our cat,
feed our cat, feed our cat.

This is the way we feed our cat
so early Wednesday morning.

Every day there are chores to do.
So get them done and have some fun.

Now, this is the way we clean our room, clean our room, clean our room.

This is the way we clean our room so early Thursday morning.

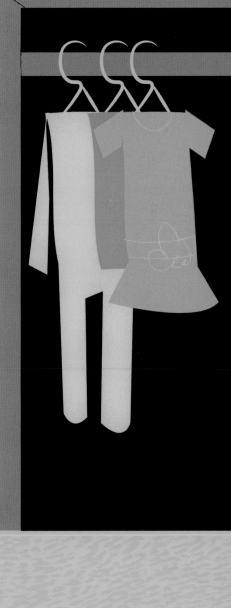

This is the way we brush our teeth,
brush our teeth, brush our teeth.

This is the way we brush our teeth
so early Friday morning.

Every day there are chores to do.
So get them done and have some fun.

Now, this is the way we sweep the floor,
sweep the floor, sweep the floor.

This is the way we sweep the floor
so early Saturday morning.

This is the way we pick up toys,
pick up toys, pick up toys.

This is the way we pick up toys
so early Sunday morning.

Yes, every day there are chores to do.

So get them done and have some fun.

SONG LYRICS
These Are the Chores We Do

Every day there are chores to do.
So get them done and have some fun.

Now this is the way we make our bed,
make our bed, make our bed.

This is the way we make our bed
so early every morning.

This is the way we tie our shoes,
tie our shoes, tie our shoes.

This is the way we tie our shoes
so early Monday morning.

Every day there are chores to do.
So get them done and have some fun.

Now, this is the way we zip our coat,
zip our coat, zip our coat.

This is the way we zip our coat
so early Tuesday morning.

This is the way we feed our cat,
feed our cat, feed our cat.

This is the way we feed our cat
so early Wednesday morning.

Every day there are chores to do.
So get them done and have some fun.

Now, this is the way we clean our room,
clean our room, clean our room.

This is the way we clean our room
so early Thursday morning.

This is the way we brush our teeth,
brush our teeth, brush our teeth.

This is the way we brush our teeth
so early Friday morning.

Every day there are chores to do.
So get them done and have some fun.

Now, this is the way we sweep the floor,
sweep the floor, sweep the floor.

This is the way we sweep the floor
so early Saturday morning.

This is the way we pick up toys,
pick up toys, pick up toys.

This is the way we pick up toys
so early Sunday morning.

Yes, every day there are chores to do.
So get them done and have some fun.

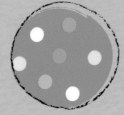

These Are the Chores We Do

Hip Hop
Drew Temperante

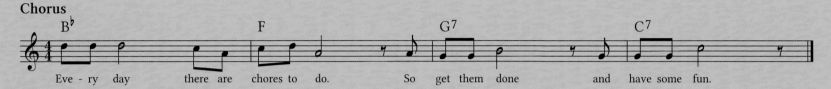

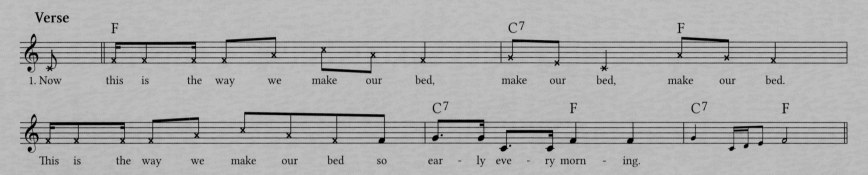

Chorus

Every day there are chores to do. So get them done and have some fun.

Verse

1. Now this is the way we make our bed, make our bed, make our bed. This is the way we make our bed so early every morning.

Verse 2
This is the way we tie our shoes,
tie our shoes, tie our shoes.
This is the way we tie our shoes
so early Monday morning.

Chorus

Verse 3
Now, this is the way we zip our coat,
zip our coat, zip our coat.
This is the way we zip our coat
so early Tuesday morning.

Verse 4
This is the way we feed our cat,
feed our cat, feed our cat.
This is the way we feed our cat
so early Wednesday morning.

Chorus

Verse 5
Now, this is the way we clean our room,
clean our room, clean our room.
This is the way we clean our room
so early Thursday morning.

Verse 6
This is the way we brush our teeth,
brush our teeth, brush our teeth.
This is the way we brush our teeth
so early Friday morning.

Chorus

Verse 7
Now, this is the way we sweep the floor,
sweep the floor, sweep the floor.
This is the way we sweep the floor
so early Saturday morning.

Verse 8
This is the way we pick up toys,
pick up toys, pick up toys.
This is the way we pick up toys
so early Sunday morning.

Chorus

23

GUIDED READING ACTIVITIES

1. Chores are jobs that people do. What chores do you have at home?

2. The monsters have chores on Monday and other days. Can you name the days of the week?

3. The monsters tie their shoes and zip their coats. Can you tie your shoes and zip your coat? Try it. How long does it take? Do you need help?

TO LEARN MORE

Bracken, Beth. *Henry Helps Clean His Room*. North Mankato, MN: Picture Window Books, 2013.

Clanton, Ben. *The Table Sets Itself*. New York: Walker–Bloomsbury, 2013.

Rissman, Rebecca. *Cleaning Up*. Chicago: Heinemann, 2014.

Rissman, Rebecca. *Should Wendy Walk the Dog? Taking Care of Your Pets*. Chicago: Heinemann, 2013.